Peter and the Pebble

Peter and the Pebble

by Paul Hunt

First Printing: 2021

ISBN: 9798450956886

Imprint: Independently Published

Images created using StoryboardThat.com

This is Peter.

Say hello to Peter.

Peter has lots of adventures.

This adventure is about a very remarkable pebble.

Turn over to read all about what happens…

It was a bright, beautiful morning.

The sky was blue and Peter was playing in the garden…

…when he noticed something on the lawn.

It was something small and rather round.

What could it be?

Peter crouched down to get a closer look.

It looked liked a precious jewel, waiting to be noticed.

Peter was captivated.

Peter picked up the mystery object.

It was a lonely little pebble.

Peter held the pebble in his hand, inspecting it carefully.

It felt as smooth as silk, and it seemed to shimmer in the sunlight.

There were so many beautiful colours.

Peter was delighted with his precious new find.

It was the most beautiful thing he had ever seen.

He promised to himself to take good care of the pebble,

then proudly went back to the house to show Mother what he had found.

"Mother, look what I've found in the garden," said Peter excitedly.

"Ooh, isn't that a lovely pebble, Peter?" said Mother, with a warm smile.

"Yes, and I'm going to look after it," Peter said. "His name is Pebble."

"You're such a good boy, Peter", said Mother.

Peter and Pebble stayed together all day.

It was such a happy day.

But then...

…at bedtime, Mother found Peter in his room.

Peter was crying.

"Whatever's the matter, my dear Peter?", said Mother.

Peter knelt on the floor.

He was pointing at Pebble.

"I dropped Pebble", said Peter tearfully.

"But I promised I would take good care of him."

Peter looked very sad.

"Let's take a look at him, shall we?" said Mother.

Mother picked up Pebble while Peter watched.

She then gently handed Pebble over to Peter.

"See, Peter? Pebble is just fine," said Mother.

Peter rolled Pebble over in his hands.

He then gasped, "Oh, but look!"

There was a small mark on the pebble.

"Pebble has been hurt," said Peter.

He then tried to wipe the mark from Pebble.

But it was no use, and Peter sobbed again

"I know what to do", said Mother.

She gently took Pebble from Peter's hand, and turned to leave the room.

"Now you just wait there for a moment, Peter", she said.

Mother then left the room with Pebble.

A few minutes later, Mother returned.

In her hand was Pebble, but he looked different.

Pebble was now wrapped in a tiny white bandage.

"This should make him all better," Mother said.

Peter stayed with Pebble all evening.

He wanted to take extra good care of Pebble.

At bedtime, Peter lovingly placed Pebble under his pillow.

As Peter went to sleep, he smiled, knowing that Pebble would be better soon.

Peter woke early the following morning.

He had slept well.

He couldn't wait to say hello to Pebble.

So he lifted up his pillow to greet his friend.

Pebble's bandage was gone!

Peter suddenly felt upset again.

He took Pebble in his hands and turned him over,

searching for where the mark had been.

The mark was gone!

Peter jumped for joy!

Pebble was all better now.

Peter pressed Pebble gently against his face and smiled a huge smile.

Mother watched Peter and Pebble from the doorway.

She was also smiling brightly.

"Didn't I tell you he would be all better soon?" she said.

"But how did you know, Mother?" said Peter.

"I just had a feeling," said Mother with a wink and a knowing smile.

She then left without saying anything else.

Peter was a such happy boy.

He was so happy he could cry!

THE END

Dear Reader.

Do you have any ideas why Mother knew that Pebble would get better?

Are there any lessons to be learnt from this story?

Until we return with Peter's next adventure, be safe and be happy.